TECWYN, THE LAST OF
THE WELSH DRAGONS

TECWYN, THE LAST OF THE WELSH DRAGONS

By Mary Dawson

Illustrated by Ingrid Fetz

PARENTS' MAGAZINE PRESS   NEW YORK

To Pamela, Tim, Dougal and Rosalind—my critics

CONTENTS

I
A VERY SMALL DRAGON

One day, in a valley deep in the heart of the Welsh mountains, a dragon was born. All his relatives had lived and died in the time of St. George when dragon-slaying was a popular sport. But this particular dragon egg had rested forgotten in the darkest and deepest lake, which lay in the long purple shadows of the mountains.

Nearby was the sleepy little village of Pennyben. It was a quiet spot where people went for their holidays, and nothing much ever happened there. Then suddenly the grinding noise of machinery shattered the peace of the valley. First came men with measuring tapes and poles. They were busy all day marking the site of the first atomic power plant to be built in Wales. Then bulldozers, cranes and trucks rumbled through the village. The work went on, and part of the lake had to be drained to make room for more buildings.

As the waters sank, the rays of the sun warmed the forgotten egg. Weeks and months went by, and then, one morning, the egg cracked and the last dragon of Wales emerged.

All day the little creature stayed in the hollow, waiting for the noise of the machines to stop. Then, very slowly, he crawled out, shaking the last bits of eggshell from his back, and looked around him.

Now instinct is strong in all animals, but particularly in dragons. Not far from the spot where he had climbed out, the men had left the remains of a fire where they had boiled a kettle of water for tea. The coals were still glowing in the evening light and, with the natural hunger of any newly-born animal, the small dragon crawled over towards the food, for of course he was a fire-breathing dragon. To breathe fire he had to eat the food that makes it. The stuff smelled right and instinct drew him towards it.

The glowing embers slid down his corrugated throat deliciously, and he sighed with content as the first smoke puffed out through his little nostrils. But, just like most babies, he did not know when to stop. By the time he had eaten all the ashes, his stomach was rumbling horribly and he crawled away into a little hole under a tree to try to sleep it off.

For a long time after dark there was a glow coming from the hole where the poor dragon lay panting with indigestion. But at last he fell asleep. His mouth shut. And it was dark on the lakeside.

It was there that Megan and Hugh found him next morning on their way to school. They were Thomas Morgan's children. Engine Morgan, their father, was in charge of the work on the atomic power plant. Megan had two dark plaits, just long enough to be pulled by her ten-year-

old brother. She had a funny gap in her top row of teeth, for she was eight and waiting for the new ones to come through. Hugh was taller than his sister, and his black hair and thick dark eyebrows made him a small shadow of his father.

Probably Megan would never have noticed the dragon, but for the huge yawn he gave as he woke up. The puff of smoke rose, twisting in the air, just in front of the children. "Look, Hugh!" she called to him. "Someone's left a fire burning; we'd better stamp it out."

Hugh was just going to bring his feet down with a thump when the dragon opened his eyes and quickly jumped out of his hole. Both children stood quite still. "Gosh, Megan! Whatever is it?" said Hugh. "A lizard?" The little dragon lay panting with fright, and his smoke jerked upwards at each breath he took.

Megan stepped nearer and bent down to look at the funny little creature. "Oh, Hugh! Could it be a real Welsh dragon? Oh, how marvellous that would be! Come and look, he's got lovely tiny wings, and he's red, just like the dragon on our Welsh flag. Oh, you darling little thing!" and Megan gazed at their wonderful discovery.

Hugh was on his knees by now, but he could hardly believe his eyes. Long ago, dragons had been common in Wales. Hugh had seen lots of pictures in fairy-tale books, and on the flags that flapped from high flagstaffs on special days. But now, just in front of him, a small fiery-looking dragon was squinting out of bright, frightened eyes.

"But, Megan, there *aren't* any dragons left now. Even Gran doesn't believe in them anymore, and she's awfully old."

"Well, let's take him home, and then she'll have to!" said Megan, and put out her hand to pick up the dragon. "Ouch! He's hot," she shouted, and put him down again very quickly.

"I'm sorry," said a small, frightened voice, "but I can't help it. It's my food, you know."

"Oh! Then you're a real fire-breathing dragon, aren't you?" said Hugh.

"Oh, yes, he must be if he's a Welsh dragon. But where-ever did you come from, and what's your name?" said Megan.

"I climbed out of that hole over there," said the little dragon, "but I don't know anything else about me at all." There was a sizzling sound, as two tears rolled out of his eyes onto his hot cheeks.

"We must think of a name for you, and you must come and live with us until you're a bit older." Hugh talked quietly to reassure the frightened little creature.

"Yes!" said Megan. "You might get hurt if you stay

here, because they're building an atomic power station, and there are lots of trucks and bulldozers working. You're so small they might not notice you."

The school bell began to ring impatiently.

"Come on, Hugh, we must hurry. Let's put him in my lunch box and take him with us," Megan said, pushing her sandwiches into her pocket. She pulled on her thick leather gloves and lifted the dragon into her lunch box and Hugh helped him to curl up.

"Is that all right?" said Hugh.

"Yes, thank you," and a tuft of smoke curled into the air. Then the children hurried off along the road to school.

II
COAL FOR COWS

At present the dragon was far too big a secret to share with anyone else, so the children put the lunch box in the corner of the boiler house, at the back of the school.

"There you are, you'll be quite safe. We'll come and see you at lunch time," said Hugh as he piled some coal around the box, so that it would not be seen from the door.

"Lunch time, did you say?" and the little dragon's tongue darted out and picked up a piece of coal, which disappeared quickly into his mouth.

"Yes, we have lunch at twelve; we'll come then. But you musn't eat too much of this coal you know, or you'll set fire to the building with your breath," said Megan.

The dragon curled up in his box and shut his eyes.

Sleep was the next best thing to food for a young animal.

The teachers were just calling the roll as Hugh and Megan ran to join their classes. Soon both were busy with lessons. Hugh was learning how to do fractions, and Megan was taught about cattle cake and grazing for cows. It was far more fun thinking about dragons, and when Miss Lloyd asked Megan what cows would be fed on besides grass, she answered at once, "Coal." All the children laughed, but Miss Lloyd told her to attend to the lesson, and Megan felt rather ashamed and was glad that Hugh had not been there to hear her.

At last it was lunch time, and the two children hurried down to the boiler house to see their secret pet. The dragon puffed out two gray wisps of smoke in his excitement at seeing them.

"Are you all right?" said Megan, bending down to talk to him.

"You've eaten an awful lot of coal," Hugh pointed to the gap in the wall that they had built round the little animal.

"I felt hungry when I thought about lunch. And I mustn't let my fire go out, you know. I feel lovely and warm inside now, and very . . . . very . . . . sleepy." He blinked once or twice, rumbled quietly, and was asleep again.

"Good," said Megan. "We'll fetch him after school and take him home to show Mum and Dad. Won't they be surprised?"

Hugh was filling up the gap in the wall of coal. "Yes, and just think of having a real Welsh dragon in the house."

The dragon slept on. Food and sleep, sleep and food, that was all a baby dragon needed. The school children came out into the playground, and ran about shouting and singing. Teachers walked past the boiler house on their way to their lessons. But nobody knew the secret that it held, except for Engine Morgan's two excited children.

When school was over, Hugh fetched the dragon from

his hiding place, while Megan made sure that nobody followed him. Luckily it had begun to rain and the children were all in a hurry to get home to their tea. Even those who usually walked home with Megan and Hugh did not wait when Megan said she was not ready yet. With the lunch box safely tucked under his raincoat, Hugh joined Megan at the end of the school lane. As they walked they began to tell the little dragon about their home.

"Dad works at the site. He's an engineer. That's why they call him Engine Morgan. I'm going to be an engineer, too, when I grow up," said Hugh.

"Our Uncle's called Bread Davis, he makes lovely bread. But it's not as good as Mum's Welsh cakes. It's a pity dragons eat such dull stuff," said Megan. "Welsh cakes are marvellous with lots of butter dripping down the sides."

Suddenly, Hugh stopped. "Megan, you know the picture in the fairy-tale book Grannie gave us with the huge red dragon that rescued the princess from the magician?"

"Yes, I know. It's a lovely one, and the dragon's all fiery. His scales shine and he looks very proud and handsome," said Megan.

"Well, he's called Tecwyn, and I think that would be a grand name for *our* dragon. He'll grow up to be just as handsome and do brave deeds like the one in the story."

"That's a wonderful idea. But we'd better see what he

thinks first, hadn't we?"

Hugh lifted his coat so that he could see the little dragon as he spoke. "Would you like to be called Tecwyn?" he said.

"Tecwyn, Tecwyn . . . ." said the dragon softly to himself. "Tecwyn of Pennyben." He rolled the name off his tongue and rumbled with pleasure. "Yes. That's my name," he decided.

By this time the children were walking along a steep narrow road with rows of small houses, each with a tiny strip of backyard. Some were dug and planted, others were just dumping grounds for bicycles, tin baths for the blackened miners, and coal to make the water hot. At the end of the road, next to the chapel, stood the Morgans' home, "Bala," and the children went up to the back door. Mrs. Morgan called to them as she came along the path carrying a basket of washing. Megan was just in time to open the door for her mother.

"Hello, Mum! We've got a surprise for you," said Hugh.

"Well, love, I hope it's a nice one. I've done a great big wash and not a bit of it dry yet. This afternoon's rain saw to that." Mrs. Morgan put down her basket with a sigh.

"Poor Mum!" said Megan. The children went into the hall to hang up their things, while Mrs. Morgan put the

washing on a line in the kitchen. By the time the last shirt
was up, Hugh and Megan were ready to show Tecwyn to
their mother. Carefully they put the lunch box down by
the fire, just in case any sparks should go the wrong way.

"Come on, Tecwyn," whispered Hugh. "You can climb
out now."

"Look, Mum," said Megan, as the tiny dragon stretched
his stiff legs, and climbed on to the hearthrug.

"Whatever is it?" shrieked Mrs. Morgan stepping back-
wards into the laundry basket.

"This is Tecwyn, our real Welsh dragon. He's an
orphan, and he climbed out of a hole by the new site, and

he's fire-breathing, and he . . . ." began Hugh, but Megan was determined to tell some of the story herself.

"He's very lonely and he needs a home and he eats coal and please, Mum, can we keep him?" she said, as fast as she could get the words out.

By this time Mrs. Morgan had climbed out of the laundry basket and recovered enough to look at this extraordinary pet that her children had brought into the house. She gazed at Tecwyn, unable to believe her eyes.

"Pinch me, Hugh. I can't see straight. Is it a lizard you've brought home? I can't stand snakes and lizards that wriggle about on the ground." Her son obliged with a pinch. But that did not help Mrs. Morgan. She still found herself staring at a creature that looked just as if it had dropped off the flag that floated in the air on St. David's day from the castle tower.

"The last time I saw anything like this was when we were reading about the red dragon in your fairy book. Why, it's even got smoke coming out of its nostrils!"

Sparks from the dragon's breath chased each other to join the flames from the fire.

"That's why we've called him Tecwyn, Mum. Isn't he beautiful, and just think of our village having its own Welsh dragon." Megan picked up a lump of coal and held it out to Tecwyn.

"Why, you dear little thing," said Mrs. Morgan. "Indeed you must stay with us. If coal is all you need, that will be easy. Coal almost grows in Wales."

Tecwyn crunched the lump that Megan had given him. His eyes flashed as he listened to this good news. "I think I could be quite useful when I'm a bit bigger," he whispered, as if he were not quite used to the sound of his own voice yet.

"Could he sleep in the coal shed, Mum?" said Hugh. "He wouldn't take up much room."

"Yes of course he can," said Mrs. Morgan. "But you're only a baby dragon, so off with you to bed now. Megan, go and tuck him in. My goodness me, whatever next! A real Welsh dragon living in our house! Just wait till Dad gets home; he'll think we're teasing him."

By the time Engine Morgan's motor-bike could be heard purring up the road, potatoes and sausages were sizzling brown in the frying pan.

The children stopped him before he reached the gate, and both started talking at once. He caught a muddle of words: "Dragon . . . . smoke . . . . coal . . . . very tiny . . . . Tecwyn . . . ." But the thing he heard most clearly was: "He's going to live with us."

III
NEWS FOR PENNYBEN

Engine Morgan was a very understanding father and did not stop to argue. He put away his bike and went into the house after Megan and Hugh, following the delicious smell that came from the kitchen.

Having received no satisfactory answer yet, the children started all over again, but Mrs. Morgan managed to make herself heard first.

"Well, Thomas, have the children told you we've got a new boarder?" she said, as she began to share out the sausages and potatoes onto the four plates.

"Now, Gwen, love, let's hear about it, and one at a time please," said Engine Morgan.

Fortunately both children had their mouths full, so that Mrs. Morgan began the story of Tecwyn's arrival.

"Well, my goodness!" said Thomas. "We've found some pretty funny things since we began work on the site, Gwen, but I never thought we'd find a dragon. Now let's hear what you've *really* found—a lizard, a snake, or what?"

"There, Dad doesn't believe us!" said Megan, passing her plate up for a second helping. "You must finish your supper, Dad, and then we'll take you to see him."

"Honestly, Dad, he's lovely and he only eats coal, so that will be easy, won't it?" said Hugh.

"That's all right as long as the miners don't strike," said their father, entering into the joke himself now.

"Can I go and fetch Tecwyn, Mum?" said Hugh, who had gone without a second helping in order to be ready first. Mrs. Morgan nodded and smiled. In a few moments Megan followed her brother outside.

"Now, Thomas," said his wife, "remember Tecwyn is a fire-breathing dragon, so you mustn't get too close to his face or you'll be scorched."

Engine Morgan laughed and pushed his chair away from the table. "You're in the joke, too, are you, love? Oh well, I don't mind having my leg pulled, but I don't like keeping wild animals in captivity—lizards and snakes in particular."

Mrs. Morgan began to clear the table and Thomas

helped her, and then the door opened. Instead of a cold blast of air coming in, a warm puff of smoke announced the dragon's arrival. He stood between Megan and Hugh —very small, but really quite fierce, with his fiery breath coming in jets from his nostrils.

"Well, I'll be! Am I seeing things, Gwen, love? It's . . . . . . it's. . . . . ." Tall Engine Morgan shut his eyes and sat down rather suddenly in his chair.

"Dad, we told you, but you wouldn't believe us. Look at him! He's the greatest! And he needs a home, and Mum says we can keep him in the coal shed," again the story began. But there was no need to persuade their father anymore. He was soon kneeling down by the dragon, talking quietly so as not to frighten him.

"So you got left behind, did you, boyo? That's hard lines. But you needn't worry anymore. This is your home from now on, and we're very proud to have you." He held out a lump of coal, and watched, fascinated, as a red tongue scooped it up and strong teeth ground it into tasty powder.

"You'll do great things one day, Tecwyn," said Mr. Morgan, "and all the folks of Pennyben will be proud of you."

"I hope I can be useful. If only I can grow big quickly," said the dragon, puffing with excitement.

Engine Morgan stood gaping. "A *talking* dragon, too? Well this beats everything. Why didn't you tell me, Gwen? Fancy him talking, it's just impossible, why I......." and Engine Morgan rubbed his eyes, and shook himself.

"Mum wasn't surprised that he talked, were you?" said Megan. "She imagines things and tells us stories, so of course she expected him to talk."

"I suppose that's right," said her mother. "Once I realized we'd a real dragon in the house, nothing else surprised me."

"Oh look, Tecwyn," said Hugh. "You've burnt some paint off the chair."

"Oh dear," said the dragon, "I'm very sorry. My breath always gets hot after I've been eating."

"Never mind that," said Mr. Morgan, "I've had an idea. Tecwyn can be my blowtorch; that will save a lot of time and trouble when I'm painting. He can burn off the old paint, ready for me—splendid!"

"Bedtime for small dragons now," said Mrs. Morgan. "Off to the shed with you, and sleep tight, and no more coal for tonight. We don't want a fire."

Tecwyn followed the children outside, and at once the room felt a shade cooler.

"Well, Gwen! We shan't need any electric heating, I'm thinking. And you needn't worry about rainy wash-days any more, either," said Thomas.

"No, that's true. A few puffs from our dragon, and the clothes will be ready for ironing," said Gwen, as her husband pulled up a chair to the fire and lit his pipe.

"I think it's a fine thing to happen, Thomas, love. And what a pet for the children!" she added, as she put away the last cup and saucer.

So that was how Tecwyn first came to Pennyben, found a happy home with Morgan family, and spent his time eating and sleeping. He did not need much exercise at first so he was kept a deep, dark secret.

But like all babies he grew, and much faster than most. After a few months he could only just manage to lie in the coal shed, and the new load of coal had to be piled

outside in the yard. He always seemed to be hungry, and the Morgans were beginning to feel worried, for coal was expensive, and the dragon ate more and more.

As the last leaves were falling off the trees and merry puffs of smoke spiralled from the chimneys of Pennyben, Tecwyn—the *large* Welsh dragon—crunched his last mouthful of supper.

He was stretched through the hall of the house, head in

the kitchen, tail by the front door. The kitchen was the part that mattered, for he loved company.

"I'm sorry, but I'm still hungry," he said, looking hopefully at the coal scuttle. "And if my fire goes out I'll be no use at all."

It was true that he was very useful indeed now. He lit the fires with a puff of his hot breath. He burnt up leaves and garden rubbish, and scorched off old paint for Engine Morgan very efficiently. But the trouble was that he ate much more than when he was a puppy-dragon.

Megan looked out of the window at the cold, gray sky. "Oh dear!" she sighed. "It looks like snow, and then we shall need even more coal."

Tecwyn's eyes began to look suspiciously wet. Suddenly Hugh jumped up. "Why, Megan! That would be wonderful—snow, ice, frozen pipes . . . ." he shouted. "Now's the time to tell the village about Tecwyn. He'll be terrific. He can thaw pipes, and be a snowplow, and then he can be paid with coal. Tecwyn, what do you think about that? You're big enough to meet anyone now."

The dragon looked up at Hugh, sadly. "There's just one thing. I tried to fly last night, and my wings aren't any use. You see I had no one to teach me how to use them, and they've never grown properly."

"Oh, Tecwyn, you'd look silly with great big wings. Besides, you might fly away and get lost. We love you just as you are—the real Welsh dragon of Pennyben," and Megan thumped his scaly back.

"I'll do anything to earn my dinner," said the dragon. "I'll go round the village doing jobs. Why, I can even clear the railway lines if snow comes."

That night the whole family went to bed feeling much happier. Now all they needed was snow. Engine Morgan had talked about work having to stop on the site for the atomic power station if snow came. But, with Tecwyn's help, even this could go on.

IV
TECWYN EARNS HIS KEEP

For the next few days Hugh and Megan were busy draw-
ing posters. One had a huge picture of Tecwyn on it, with
smoke and sparks coming from his nostrils. Another said:
"Don't use matches, use Tecwyn." "Tecwyn—your blowtorch!" and so it went on. The posters looked fine when
the children had painted them. Engine Morgan and Gwen
helped to hang them outside on the garden wall.

"I wonder who'll be the first to see them," said Megan
that night as she climbed the stairs to go to bed.

"Ifan, the post, of course, when he comes with the
letters," said Hugh. "I'd like to see his face when he has
his first sight of Tecwyn."

Hugh was right. The first thing he heard next morning

was a hammering at the door, and Ifan Jones, the postman, shouting, "Anyone at home?"

Engine Morgan opened the door and took the letters.

"What's all this then about a dragon, Thomas? Are you having a little joke? It's not carnival time yet, you know."

"Wait till I show you, Ifan boy! He'll make Pennyben famous before we're known for our atomic power station. You see if he doesn't," and he led the way to the coal shed, where the dragon lay fast asleep, with gentle puffs of smoke coming from his nostrils.

The postman rubbed his eyes, shook his head, looked again and gasped. "What are you playing at, man? I've not touched a drop of drink or I'd think I was seeing things. Why! Our flag's dropped its dragon into your shed!" Ifan stepped over to have a closer look at the sleeping dragon. "Ah, well!" he said. "Pennyben's a wonderful place, Thomas."

"That's just it, Ifan. Tecwyn crawled out of a hollow when the lake was drained. The children found him on the way to school. I reckon he must have got left behind when his relations left. There's not been a dragon around since old St. George was busy rescuing maidens. He was quite a little fellow when the children found him. But my goodness! he's grown a lot since then. That's why we decided it was time to tell the village about him. He eats coal and it's getting expensive feeding him. But if he can earn his food by doing jobs, we'll be able to manage."

By this time the children had joined them, and Tecwyn had waked up and begun his breakfast. He did not even bother to open his eyes at first, but just stretched out his tongue to a pile of coal, and scooped up a large mouthful. He crunched so loudly that Ifan and Thomas could hardly hear themselves speak. But Ifan, the postman, had a lot of letters to deliver, and soon he hurried off, promising to tell anyone he met about the useful dragon with fire in his stomach.

Tecwyn's first job that morning was to light the fire for Mrs. Morgan. Then he went into the yard with the children to see if anyone was coming to ask for his help.

The road was busy with men and women going to work, but they were all going *down* the hill to the mine, or to the shops.

The miners wore their tin helmets, and had haversacks with their food for the shift. Women hurried along with bags, containing overalls and comfortable shoes to work in. Nobody was coming up to the house with the gay posters on the wall, and the board with "Bala" printed on it.

"Oh dear, Hugh, I *do* hope someone will come soon," Megan shivered as the north wind blew in between her plaits and down her neck.

"Ifan will tell them, don't worry," said Hugh, holding his hands near Tecwyn's mouth to catch some of his warmth. The dragon stayed just inside the wall, where he could watch the gate.

After what seemed to them all an age, their uncle, Bread Davis, drove up in his van. A glorious smell of hot loaves drifted out into the cold air. "Hullo! Hullo! Megan, what's all this about dragons?" and there he stopped, as Tecwyn peered out of the gate, sniffing the delicious smell.

"My word, but you're a whopper, aren't you!" said Mr. Davis, gazing at the dragon in amazement.

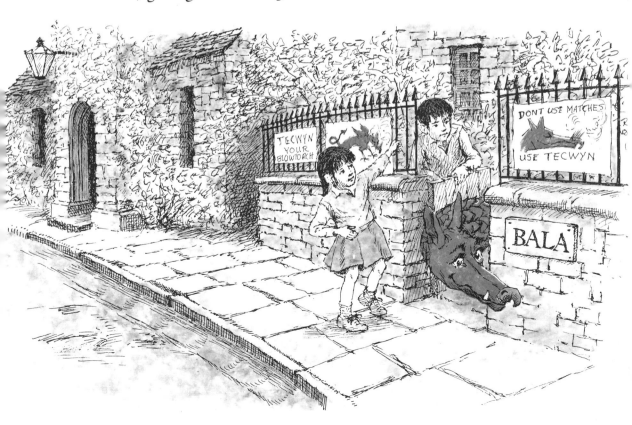

"He's ever so useful, Uncle. He can light fires."

". . . . . Burn off old paint."

". . . . . Thaw frozen pipes." The children recited the dragon's virtues in turn.

"That'll come in useful by the look of it," said Bread Davis, pointing to the dirty gray sky.

"Two big loaves, please," called Mrs. Morgan. "Isn't he a beauty?" as she came over to take the bread from the baker.

"That'll be a tale to deliver with my bread round," said Mr. Davis, slamming the door of his van. Then he drove off.

The children watched their uncle drive on up the hill, and when they turned round again they saw a crowd of people starting up the road from the center of Pennyben. In front came Mr. Pugh, the Chapel minister, hatless and hurrying, his face rosy and red. Behind him followed a crowd, and among them was fat Butcher Evans, his striped apron flapping in the wind, his chopper still in his hand.

"Oh, goody! goody!" shouted Megan. "They're coming at last." Hugh opened the gate, and with Tecwyn between them they stood and waited.

"Well! Well! This is a marvel indeed!" said the minister, puffing and panting as he arrived first at the gate of Bala. "A dragon in Pennyben, and a Welsh dragon, too."

He turned to the butcher, who quickly put his chopper behind his back, when he saw the dragon's frightened expression. "Evans, my friend, you have seen a miracle. A dragon standing on a street in Pennyben."

"Biggest critter I ever saw," said the butcher. "And that's saying something."

Gradually the crowd gathered round, and Megan and Hugh shut Tecwyn inside their gate so that he could be seen but not prodded by inquisitive fingers. Once again Megan and Hugh told their story to a silent crowd, who did not want to miss a single word.

Orders for the dragon's help came in all day and there was no more need to worry about his food. By evening all the people of Pennyben who could come had seen Tecwyn, and in the streets there was talk of little else.

Just as Megan was putting out the empty milk bottles for her mother that night she felt something wet on her cheek. "It's snowing!" she shouted, and ran indoors.

In the morning there was a thick layer of snow everywhere except on the roof of the shed. It had little chance of settling there, for Tecwyn's breath kept the shed warm and toasty. There was a drift of snow on the path up to the front door.

"Hi! Where's our dragon?" shouted Ifan, the postman, as he stamped up to the door with the snow coming almost over his rubber boots. Tecwyn heard Ifan and wriggled his long, scaly body out of the shed, and gave a huge puff. As if by magic, the snow turned into a trickling stream and rolled away in front of the postman.

"That's the style, boyo!" said Ifan. "How about finishing the round for me?"

"You can ride on my back and show me the way. I won't be too hot with all this snow about," said the dragon, delighted to find himself being really useful at last. Megan and Hugh came out of the house wearing their boots, thick sweaters and gloves. They ran to join the dragon and the postman.

"Jump up, all of you!" said Tecwyn. Ifan perched himself in front, with the children a little further down the long, scaly back which was just pleasantly warm.

"All aboard and away we go!" said Tecwyn, and off they went. A huge breakfast when he woke up had given the dragon a roaring fire inside and he had plenty of fiery breath for his job as a snowplow. People in the streets of Pennyben cheered as he went by. Many of them stopped, amazed to see the snow being turned into running water. The post round was finished in record time, and children everywhere were thrilled with the new "mail truck."

"What next?" asked the dragon when the mail bag was empty.

A railway porter came hurrying up to him. "The station master wants you urgently, Tecwyn," he said. "The express to Brecon's due to leave in five minutes and the line's blocked with snow."

The dragon snorted and flicked his tail. "Righto! Then I'll come round at once, but I'll need some more food to keep my fire going first."

"There's plenty in the station yard," said the porter. "But please hurry. The express has never been late yet, and it would be a dreadful thing to happen."

Tecwyn hurried off, with the children riding on his back and the porter running alongside. The anxious station master was waiting for them, watch in hand. He looked very agitated. But as soon as Tecwyn appeared he smiled with relief.

"Oh! It *is* good to see you, Tecwyn," he said. "We've got steam up and everyone's getting very impatient. This snow is a great nuisance. I don't know what we should have done without you. The snowplow's clearing the other line."

Tecwyn was busily refuelling himself from a truck on a siding, crunching noisily all the time. "That'll do for a while," he said, as he emptied a second truck of its load of coal. His smoke puffed into the winter air, and sparks played tag with each other as they floated up into the clear sky. The dragon stepped down in front of the engine, took a deep breath and then blew at the snow on the line in front of him. The guard blew his whistle and they started off.

Tecwyn kept a safe distance from the engine so that his beautiful tail would not be damaged.

As the wonderful dragon streaked along, with sparks flying where his claws struck the metal rails, he almost seemed to leave the ground. On the straight stretches, every now and then, he actually glided, and the children felt they were flying. The passengers cheered, and Hugh and Megan, still on his broad, scaly back, felt warm and happy and *very* proud of their wonderful dragon.

V
FIRE! FIRE!

All that winter Tecwyn kept the village clear of snow, and he was never short of food. He did once try coal dust, but it gave him hiccups so he did not try it again. He had no worries at all, and everybody loved him. And—if possible—he was more handsome than ever. He was now full grown and every scale along his back gleamed so that it dazzled people to look at him.

The cold weather seemed to go on for a very long time that winter. But at last the buds on the trees began to swell, the snow disappeared, and snowdrops lined the front path to the door of the Morgans' home.

Work at the power station was nearing completion. The huge buildings stood tall and splendid side by side and surrounded by a network of pipes. Down by the lake, giant machines filtered the water free of fishes, twigs and leaves, before it began its long journey through miles of piping. Inside the buildings engineers, led by Engine Morgan, were very busy completing the final stages before the great station could begin work.

One morning, Tecwyn was doing a useful bit of soldering at the station, when he heard Engine Morgan talking to some of his mates. "It looks as if we'll be counting the lumps of coal very soon," he said. "All but two mines are on strike now." He sounded very worried, and his forehead had a strange wrinkled look that Tecwyn recognized. The dragon moved a bit closer.

"Hello, Tecwyn. I'm afraid we're in trouble. I don't know what we're going to do about your food if the miners go on with their strike."

"Are they having a holiday?" said Tecwyn, puzzled. When he first arrived Mrs. Morgan had said that coal "grew" in Wales; so why need he worry all of a sudden?

Mr. Morgan explained to him that food was getting so expensive that the miners could no longer pay for what they needed, and they had decided to stop work until their wages were raised. That would mean a very serious coal shortage. Already stocks were low.

As the days went by, Tecwyn's wages went down, too.

He had less and less coal, and every night he went to bed hungry.

Then one day a dreadful thing happened. He found that his fire had gone out, and he could not blow one wisp of smoke. No smoke meant no work, and no one in the village had any coal to spare.

When Megan went out to see Tecwyn one morning before school, she found him lying in a corner of the shed, shrunken to only half his usual size. His scales were dull and wrinkled, and his skin was much too big for him. He did not even look up when she called. Megan ran over to where he was lying and knelt down.

"It's no good, Megan," he murmured. "I've tried to manage on one meal a day, but now my fire's gone out; I'm no use to anybody anymore." And he tried to sniff back the giant tears that were just about to roll down his cheeks. But this time, with no fire to dry them, they went on and on falling, until Megan began to cry, too.

This would never do. She stroked his head, blew her nose hard, and then said, "I'll fetch Mum and Dad; *they'll* know what to do. Don't worry, Tecwyn, I know it will be all right." Then she ran into the house.

"Mum! Dad! Come quickly! Tecwyn's terribly ill, he's starving. We must *do* something! His fire's gone out!" she shouted. Hugh rushed out and was horrified to see the famous dragon looking like a dried-up orange.

Mr. and Mrs. Morgan were soon at the children's side, listening to Tecwyn as he began all over again to say how sorry he was. A small pool of tears had collected round him and he was a very sad sight indeed.

It was Mr. Morgan who had the idea. "What about oil?" he said. "Lots of people use it for their heating instead of coal, so why not Tecwyn?" The others thought it a wonderful idea, and the dragon, who was hungry enough to eat anything rather than lie there being useless, agreed to try it.

Engine Morgan went off on his motor-bike to fetch as large a drum of oil as he could carry. Hugh and Megan stayed with Tecwyn. They were far too worried to go to school that day. As they sat by their beloved dragon they told him stories of the funny things that the pantomime dragon—made of ten people—had done, in the carnival last year, twisting its way through the village leading the procession. They even managed to make him laugh, though the sound his loose scales made as they rattled was horrible to hear.

When Engine Morgan returned, the children helped him to carry the oil drum into the yard. Mrs. Morgan brought a huge bowl into which they poured the thick, yellow oil, and Megan tied an old tablecloth round

Tecwyn's neck, just in case he spilled any.

"Try it, Tecwyn, old fellow," said Mr. Morgan, dipping his finger into the bowl and letting the dragon have a lick. "It may make you feel better." The poor old shadow of the real, beautiful Tecwyn dragged himself to the bowl, and then shuffled round it, sniffing all the time.

"We'll leave you in peace for a while," said Mr. Morgan. "Come along, all of you!" and he led the way into the house. Megan helped her mother with the cooking, and Hugh peeled the potatoes, while their father went off to work rather later than usual.

Suddenly Megan shouted, "I can smell smoke! Hoorah! Tecwyn must be better." And she ran outside, quite forgetting that her hands were sticky from the pastry she was making. There certainly was smoke—all over the yard it drifted, and flames were coming from the shed. Megan rushed to find Tecwyn, shouting to her mother and Hugh to come and help. The poor dragon just managed to get out of the shed before a huge flame shot up into the sky.

Hugh was already calling the fire station, while Mrs. Morgan, helped by neighbors who had seen the smoke, made a chain with buckets of water which they passed to and fro.

Megan stayed beside Tecwyn, his huge head resting on her lap as he told her what had happened.

"I had just sipped my first mouthful of that queer, yellow stuff, when I felt as if I were bursting. It was terrible! There were flames all around me, yet I was still cold inside. There must have been a spark left in my stomach after all. I don't think oil is any good for dragons," he sobbed. "I'm sorry I'm such a nuisance to everybody. Oh dear! What *am* I going to do?" and poor Tecwyn's tears began to soak Megan's dress. She held his head in her arms. She had not been able to do this since he was a puppy-dragon, but now he was small and wrinkled and so pathetic, that it was quite easy.

By this time Chief Fire Officer Pritchard and his firemen were playing their hoses onto the shed. Little by little the flames died down, and finally disappeared, leaving a mess of smoking wet rubble, and not one lump of coal.

When their work was all done, Chief Officer Pritchard and his men sat down for a minute to drink the tea that Mrs. Morgan had brought for them.

"What happened then, Tecwyn?" said Mr. Pritchard. "It's not bonfire night, you know." When Megan explained that they had tried feeding Tecwyn on oil, he understood and was very sorry. "We'll have to look round for a few pieces of coal for him. We can't have him ill. Why, the power station is due to be opened by the Queen next week, and she must see the dragon of Pennyben," he said.

That night everyone in the village brought as much coal as they could spare. Many of them shivered without a fire rather than let Tecwyn suffer, for they all loved their Welsh dragon. And so he slept with at least a smouldering fire in his stomach, and that was something. But he had too little heat inside him to do any work.

VI
MEGAN HAS AN IDEA

By the end of the week Tecwyn began to feel poorly
again; his meals had become smaller, although the people
of Pennyben tried to give him enough. There were not
many chimneys still smoking in the village, but even so,
the few lumps of coal that came to Tecwyn were hardly
enough to warm his insides.

One evening when Engine Morgan went to give the
dragon a shovelful of coal, he found him shivering so
much his scales made a noise like someone playing a xylo-
phone. It was dreadful to be unable to help the poor
dragon, but there just was not enough fuel to go round.
Mr. Morgan put the little pile of coal in front of the
hungry dragon.

"I'm sorry, Tecwyn lad," he said. "I'll try and get you some more by tonight, but it's a bad job and no mistake. All the pits are idle, and nearly all the coal scuttles in Pennyben are empty." The dragon nodded his head. He quite understood, and did not blame anybody in Pennyben. But he thought those miners had had a long enough holiday.

Megan and Hugh were miserable. Their schoolwork was getting worse and worse, and they found it impossible to do difficult problems about tons and hundredweights of coal, because it always made them think of poor Tecwyn who needed it so badly.

Their father decided it would be a good idea to take their minds off the dragon, if only for a while. He had promised that they should be shown the station when it was ready to be opened, and that was in a few days time.

"How would you like to have a look around the power station this evening?" he asked them. "It won't help Tecwyn to see you moping around the place. He feels just as miserable as we do, and that makes five of us."

The children were thrilled. This was something they had looked forward to for ages, and it would be a marvellous thing to tell their classes about.

"Yes please, Dad," said Hugh, "we'd love to. Can we see the fuel store, and look at the bars of uranium?"

"Yes, I expect so," said their father. "Go along to Mr. James and tell him I sent you. He promised he'd take you round when I gave the word. I've got to go now; there's an important meeting about the opening ceremony, and there's lots to be fixed up. See you later, and don't ask *too* many questions or you'll be there all night." Engine Morgan put on his coat, and in a moment he set off for his meeting. He was one of the people who were to be presented to Her Majesty, and for weeks Gwen had been fussing about which tie he should wear for this important occasion. He smiled to himself as he thought about it, and decided that probably the Queen would not even notice.

Megan and Hugh had a last look at Tecwyn before they went to find Mr. James at the power station. The dragon was lying in a corner of the shed counting aloud. "Fifty-nine, sixty. That means ten lumps of coal for six days or six lumps for ten days, or one meal and then . . . ."

"Oh! don't, Tecwyn!" said Megan. "I'm sure we'll think of something. Just now Hugh and I are going to be shown round the power station, but we'll be back soon, and we're sure to find something for you to eat. So please don't think this is the last food you'll ever get." Megan found it hard to look as cheerful as she sounded.

Hugh took a broom and brushed all the coal into one pile. It looked like more that way. "There, Tecwyn!"

he said. "You can eat half of this tonight and the other half tomorrow."

"And then?" muttered the dragon, to himself.

"Don't worry about the next day until it comes, that's what Mum always says," said Hugh. "Goodbye now!" and the children shut the door of the shed and ran off.

Mr. James met them at the gate of the station, because he had had a message from Mr. Morgan that they were on their way.

"Hullo! A grand tour is it?" and he laughed and let the children through the gate where the police sergeant was on duty.

"You'll be very proud of your dad on Saturday," he said. "The Queen might give him a medal, I shouldn't wonder," and he led the way towards a building where huge generators throbbed and hummed. The children had to hurry to keep up with his long strides. They gazed at the gigantic pipes and engines in the well, below the gallery where they were walking. The noise became even louder.

"Goodness! I shouldn't like to work down there," said Hugh. "It's so noisy."

Soon they passed through two pairs of swinging doors, and it became quieter again. This was the control room. The first thing Megan noticed was a ticking sound, rather

like a quiet but regular typewriter at work. She listened until she had discoverd where the sound came from, and then went over to a machine which was feeding out a long strip of paper.

"What's this for, Mr. James? There are numbers on it, and it seems to be going on and on forever." She watched the paper which was getting longer and longer.

"That tells the temperature of the reactors. Those are in the big round buildings where the heat is being made. If it gets too hot or too cold, an alarm bell rings to warn us," said Mr. James.

At a desk sat a man writing. By his side was a rack of telephones, one of which was red. Hugh pointed to it.

"Why is it red? For danger?" he asked, going nearer to the desk.

"It's a fire telephone, and you can call any part of the station in a matter of seconds on that," explained the man at the desk.

Along the walls of the control room were hundreds of switches and knobs. Every now and then lights flashed on and off. Megan and Hugh stood watching them for a moment. Megan started counting the knobs. Then she shook her head. "I've lost count. How many men are there to look after all those switches?" she said. "There must be an awful lot to learn."

"There are only four men in the control room," said Mr. James. "It would be no good having too many people in charge, or there'd be a muddle. Machines do most of the charting in here."

"Oh! This looks just like the temperature chart I had over my bed in the hospital," said Hugh, pointing to a glass case. Inside, a reel of paper revolved while a needle marked a wavy line across the surface.

"That's right, it *is* a temperature chart," said Mr. James. "There's still a lot to see yet, so we'd better go on our way." The children thanked the man at the desk, and followed Mr. James out of the swinging doors.

They went downstairs and into the open. Then they crossed a large yard which led to a long, low building. Here Mr. James stopped and took out some keys. They all went inside and he shut the door behind them.

"This is the fuel store. The uranium in here is worth thousands of pounds," he said. Then he stooped down to pull on some huge white overshoes. He answered the children's question before they had time to ask it.

"Everyone coming into this part of the shed has to wear these," he said, stepping over a cord that separated the entrance from the rest of the shed. "Then the overshoes are left here and there's no danger of radioactive dust being carried outside. That's dust that might make you ill if there's too much of it." He bent down to open a large metal case, one of hundreds stacked in the shed.

"Is the uranium in there?" asked Megan excitedly.

"Yes. Here it is," said their guide, lifting a long bar in a metal case. "You can hold it if you like; it is in a case of a metal protecting you from it, called an alloy. But DON'T drop it, whatever you do. It's very valuable." Hugh took it in both hands, and even then was glad to return it to Mr. James. Then Megan held it before it was carefully put back into its case. Mr. James closed the lid.

"It doesn't *look* very useful. Just a metal bar," said Hugh.

"Not on its own, perhaps. But when bars of uranium are in contact with a substance called graphite—that's a bit like charcoal—it makes a terrific heat. The graphite has to be there to prevent the heat being so great that there'd be an explosion," explained Mr. James, and began to take off his overshoes. He opened the door and locked it behind them. This time they took a different direction, and approached the building where one of the reactors was.

VII
SHAKING HANDS WITH A ROBOT

This time they went in an elevator to a balcony looking down onto the biggest machines they had ever seen. Mr. James showed them how, by covering a certain part of the side of the elevator, they could stop it moving.

"That's just what they did in one of the TV shows," said Hugh. "It's like an invisible eye." Megan gazed down at the pit below, where men were walking about, reading dials, and looking at more panels of switches. It looked rather like the engine room of a huge ship.

Hugh asked Mr. James some questions about how they fed this monster, and he pointed to a special machine that fed in the bars of uranium. But Hugh noticed that Megan had become very quiet. She had a faraway look that meant that she was planning something important. This made Hugh impatient to ask her about it, and as soon as they were out of the elevator, and in the open again, he began.

"What are you planning, Megan?" he asked.

She shook her head and whispered, "Not now." Hugh understood and went on talking to Mr. James.

They were now in a room with basins, and Mr. James stopped beside a machine that looked a bit like a letter box with two slots for the letters. "We have to wash our hands here," he said. "It's a check on radioactive dust. There are paper towels for you to use and throw away." He ran water over his hands and rubbed them. The children did the same and threw the paper towels into a bin.

"Now you shake hands with a robot," said Mr. James, laughing as he pointed to the queer machine with the slots. He put in both his hands, one in each slot, and waited. After a moment he took them out again. A needle on a dial just below the slot moved a fraction of an inch and then stopped.

"Your turn next, Megan," he said. "Put your hands into the slots as I did. You'll feel metal bars holding them there. Keep them still till the robot lets go." Again, as Megan and Hugh watched, fascinated, the needle swung just a little and stopped.

Then Megan took her hands out again. "That was fun,"

she said. "I bet none of my friends at school have shaken hands with a robot."

"Now Hugh," said Mr. James, as Hugh stepped up to the machine. Hugh had only had his hands in for a second when a bell rang and a little sign flashed: "TEST INTERRUPTED."

"That means that you moved your hands a little, so the test couldn't be finished. Try again." All went well, and for the third time the needle showed them free from a dangerous amount of radioactive dust.

"That's all right. If you carry enough dust to bother about, a bell rings. Every man in this section has to check out whenever he leaves the building," said Mr. James.

As the children followed Mr. James outside, Hugh caught a look from Megan that clearly meant, "Let's go home."

"Thank you for showing us such a lot of things," said Hugh. "I think we'd better be getting back now." They all went as far as the gate together, and there Mr. James waved goodbye as the children started for home.

The moment they were out of earshot Megan began to tell Hugh her plan. "I've got it, Hugh! It was when we were in the fuel shed. I've been dying to tell you ever since."

"What do you mean, Megan?" said her brother.

"Atomic power! A few bars of uranium would keep Tecwyn going for ages. He must have some charcoal left inside him from his last meal, so that would do to control the heat." Megan was getting more and more excited as she spoke.

"But wouldn't he be dangerous with all that power inside him?" said Hugh.

"Not with his marvellous strong scales," said Megan. "And they *would* be strong again once his fire was burning well in his stomach. It's the only way to save him, and we must do it tonight."

"We could get over the fence all right with some rope if we were very careful. The night guard is usually at his post. But I wonder if Tecwyn could climb over, he's so terribly weak."

"We could lift him over if he can't manage," said Megan.

"We'll have to creep out of the house when Mum and Dad are asleep. We know the way to the fuel store now, and I'm sure Tecwyn can pick the lock with one of his claws. But we'd better warn him of our plan. Come on!" Megan and Hugh hurried along the road and as soon as they reached home they went out to the shed.

The pile of coal lay untouched, and Tecwyn's eyes rolled sadly at them, as they went in.

"We've thought of a way to make you better, Tecwyn, dear," said Megan. "But you MUST eat all this coal first, or you won't be strong enough to climb the fence."

The dragon opened his eyes a little bit wider. He wriggled his little wings and wished once more that he could fly. Climbing was such hard work when you were so long and so empty.

"We're going to see if uranium will do for your food. It's the stuff they are going to use at the station, and it gets ever so hot, and it's put with graphite, and graphite's not very different from charcoal, and you *must* still have some charcoal inside you from your last meal," Hugh explained to the dragon, who looked very puzzled by all these strange words.

"It's marvellous stuff! Ever so strong, and you'll be billowing smoke again by tomorrow, if it works. But of course it will," he added as he saw Tecwyn's eyes beginning to water.

Hugh piled up the last lot of coal in front of the dragon's long, dry nose. "We'll come for you at midnight—you can count the strokes on the church clock—then Mum and Dad are sure to be asleep. But eat up every bit of that coal, mind, or you'll be too weak to do anything." The dragon opened his mouth, and the first lump disappeared.

During supper, the children told their parents about the things they had seen, and Engine Morgan told them about the plans for the great opening ceremony on Saturday. Megan had been chosen to present Her Majesty with a bunch of roses, and Hugh was to have the honor of handing her the golden key which was to unlock the door. Mrs. Morgan at once began to worry about what Megan should wear, and whether Hugh's suit would be tidy enough. The children were not worried, but terribly excited, and anyway Mum loved having something to worry about.

There was no need to tell them twice that it was bedtime that night. Luckily Mrs. Morgan did not notice that there were very few clothes on the children's chairs. They did not mention Tecwyn to their parents that evening, in case they let out their secret.

It seemed ages before Mr. and Mrs. Morgan went to bed, and even longer before they stopped talking and put out their light. Megan and Hugh found it a hard job to keep their eyes open, but, as the first stroke of midnight sounded on the old church clock the children, still fully dressed, crept out of their bedroom and tiptoed downstairs.

VIII
JUST IN TIME

The night was dark, and Megan was glad she had remembered her flashlight. Hugh opened the door of the shed, and the long, twisty shape of the dragon wormed its way into the garden.

Tecwyn sighed. "If only I had some fire I could have shown you the way. We could have had a torchlight procession."

"We can, still, even if it's only my pocket flashlight," said Megan, shining it for Tecwyn to see. Walking carefully on the grass at the side of the concrete path, the three figures moved out of the gate and onto the road. One carried a coil of rope. There was no sound to be heard except for the screech owl hunting for his breakfast, on silent wings.

"I ate all the coal," whispered the dragon, afraid of the sound of his own voice in the silence of the dark night. "I hope I'm strong enough for the climb."

"Don't worry, we'll lift you over if you can't manage it," said Hugh, as he hurried along beside Tecwyn and his sister.

Very soon, in front of them loomed the long white fence, the concrete posts standing up like a row of teeth. Fortunately for them, there was no barbed wire, but the fence was high and difficult to climb.

"Here we are," said Hugh, stopping at the fence. He looked up and down and Megan listened. Tecwyn just looked at it and wondered how he would get over. It was no good, he decided, he would *not* be able to manage it.

When Hugh was certain that there was no one about, he uncoiled his rope, and Megan who was good at knots, made a loop at one end.

"Now, keep still, both of you! Don't make a sound. I'm going to throw the loop over the post." Tecwyn gazed hopelessly at the tall fence, and Megan waited breathlessly, as Hugh coiled the rope ready to throw. The first time he tried, the rope fell back onto the ground. But the second time the loop fell safely over the top of the post, and he pulled on it to test it.

"It's all right!" he whispered, and climbed up onto the

top of the tall fence. Then he leaned down to Megan and the dragon. "Now, Megan, you must help Tecwyn over the fence. He's not nearly as heavy as he was, poor fellow, after being half starved for so long. I'll lean down and pull while you push."

The poor dragon had his two front feet on the bottom of the fence, but could get no further. His long, shrivelled body hung behind him uselessly. He groaned, and a huge shiver went right through him.

"Come on, Megan, we'll have to haul him over loop by loop. Ready? Lift!" Little by little the children piled the loops of Tecwyn's shrunken and crinkled body over the fence. Hugh pulled and Megan pushed, panting hard with the effort. At last he was safely over. Then Megan climbed up with the help of the rope. Just as she jumped down, she let go of her flashlight, and they were in complete darkness.

"Just a minute, Hugh," she whispered, stooping to pick it up. She pressed the switch but no light shone. Then she shook it. That usually worked. But it was no use.

"Oh well," she said. "We'll have to find our way without," and she screwed up her eyes to peer into the dark night. Hugh listened for the sound of the generators which they had to pass on their way to the fuel store.

"I think it's this way," said Hugh, boldly starting off

into the blackness ahead. Megan held his hand just so that she would not get separated from him. Suddenly Tecwyn held up his head and gave a loud sniff.

"Sh! Tecwyn, you'll disturb the guard if you make such a noise," said Hugh, as they groped their way along a railing which he hoped would lead to the fuel store.

The dragon started to run, his scales rattling like pots and pans. "There's something that's just right for dragons," he rumbled between his teeth, as he hurried ahead of the children. Hugh and Megan had to run, too, and soon they could hear the humming of the engines and they knew that they had found the right way.

Once again, just as when he was a baby dragon, Tecwyn's instinct had taken over. He stopped at a pair of huge double doors, and put his nose to the keyhole and sniffed. "It's in here!" he whispered, and pushed one of his long claws into the lock and jerked the door open.

"Oh, Hugh! I think it's going to work," said Megan, hurrying into the shed, and carefully shutting the door behind them. Hugh groped about to find a switch, and luckily turned on a small pilot light, which was just enough to show them where the fuel cases were lying. There were the precious bars of uranium that might save Tecwyn's life!

"We'd better put on overshoes," said Megan, pushing

some over to Hugh and the dragon. Tecwyn had trouble in finding two pairs big enough for him, but managed it at last. He waddled about, flapping the shoes and looking very funny. As soon as the children had fastened theirs,

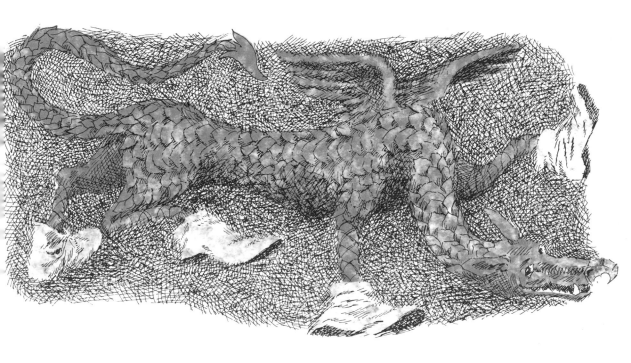

they began to open a box of fuel. Tecwyn had disappeared behind a stack of cases meanwhile, and could be heard sniffing, louder and louder. Hugh lifted the cover from the case they had opened, and Megan very, very carefully took out one bar of the wonderful fiery fuel that looked so dead and dull in her hands. "Where's Tecwyn got to?" she said.

Hugh went to the place where they had last seen him. There he was, but he looked different. Already his scales were beginning to shine again, and for the first time for many months he was looking happy.

"This is the stuff for dragons!" purred Tecwyn. "I know it. I can feel it in every one of my scales. Quick! Quick! Pop it inside!" and he opened his jaws wide enough to swallow a whole case of uranium bars at one gulp.

"Only one at once, Tecwyn, or you'll choke," said Hugh. Carefully the children lifted the bar up until it was level with the dragon's mouth, and slid it down his corrugated throat. There was a rumble as he swallowed. Then the huge mouth opened wide again.

"More, please!" Again the children heaved a precious bar up into his eager mouth, and watched as Tecwyn swallowed it down. Then—first a tiny puff, then a bigger one, and soon a steady stream of smoke rings began to spiral up towards the roof of the fuel store.

"Oh, Tecwyn, you're the greatest dragon there ever was! It's really worked. Your scales are shiny and your eyes are flashing just like they used to do. We must hurry home now, before anyone finds out we've been here," said Megan, jumping up and down. Hugh helped the dragon to take off his overshoes, and then threw all four pairs into a heap. Megan helped him to shut the case of uranium, which now had two less bars in it than when it was last checked. They hurried outside, shut the door behind them, and Tecwyn came last, NOT forgetting to lock the door behind him, because there was such important fuel for dragons inside that wonderful shed.

They reached the fence safely, and this time it was the dragon who hoisted the children over. They untied the rope and then Tecwyn gave them a ride home on his back. His breath lit the path ahead, so they had their torchlight procession after all. He crackled merrily all the way, and they took much less time than they did going to the station.

When they reached home Tecwyn wanted to wake Mr. and Mrs. Morgan to tell them the wonderful news. But the children made him promise to stay in his shed until morning, for there would have to be a great deal of explaining.

Very quietly, Megan and Hugh climbed the stairs and slipped back into bed. They were too excited to fall asleep at once, and they heard the church clock strike two before they dropped off. It was not surprising that they slept late next morning.

IX
A ROYAL VISITOR

The first thing Megan heard was her mother calling to her.

"Megan, Hugh, come and see Tecwyn! He's better— hot enough to roast the lunch! Come quickly! I don't know what's happened. It's magic, that's what it is."

The children dressed in a moment and ran downstairs. Good old Tecwyn! He had kept his secret and not told their parents yet. Thomas and Gwen were standing by the shed. Tecwyn's noble head lay outside, his scales glowing like rubies. He shone from tip to tail, and sparks flew through the door, disappearing into the air like stars from a rocket.

"Oh, Tecwyn, it *is* good to see you well again!" said Megan and looked at Hugh.

"Yes, you will be *sure* to be presented to the Queen now," said Hugh, and began to laugh. This started Megan off, and then with a mighty rumble the great dragon's laughter roared out, so that no one could hear a word. This just gave the children a moment in which to think how they should explain the secret to their surprised parents. When Tecwyn had finished roaring, and settled down again to a quiet smoke from both nostrils, Megan nodded to her brother and he began.

"It was when we were going round the station, Dad," he said.

"What was?" said his father, looking puzzled.

"I thought of it in the fuel store," added Megan.

"What did you think of, Megan, for goodness sake?" said her mother.

"Uranium." Hugh waited to see what his father would say.

"Of course you thought about uranium in the fuel store, that's where it's kept." Thomas shook his head. Really his children were being even denser than usual.

"For Tecwyn; to save his life, Dad. We had to do something, and this was our last chance. Oh! Don't be angry with us, we . . . ."

Suddenly Thomas understood it all. At first he was furious. He called the children indoors, and they all four sat

69

and talked about the whole adventure. Security was important and he felt responsible. But after the children had explained everything, and promised that they would try to earn the money for the uranium themselves "somehow," he realised that, with the fuel already burning merrily in the dragon's stomach, there was really very little he could do about it.

News travels fast, and before the men on the evening shift went off duty that night, a hundred pounds had been collected. All day television cameras and press reporters had swarmed round the station, and the money they paid for the story of the atomic dragon provided more than enough for the bars of uranium that were keeping Tecwyn happy.

At last, Saturday, the day of the opening ceremony arrived. The village was gay with flags and bunting. All the streets were lined with children and their parents, waiting to see the Queen. There was a fine red carpet for her to walk on, when she alighted from her car. But it was not as fine as the glorious red dragon of Pennyben, who stood, shining and proud at the entrance to the atomic power station. Beside him stood the engineers who had worked on the site, and Engine Morgan stood at the front.

When the Queen arrived, she stopped to talk to Thomas and Tecwyn for a whole ten minutes, which made all the

arrangements run five minutes late. At the door of the
station, Megan, in her Welsh dress and tall hat, curt-
seyed to the Queen and gave her a beautiful bouquet of
red rosebuds. Hugh bowed—as he had done so many
times before when Megan was practising her curtsey—and
handed the golden key to Her Majesty. Mr. Morgan was
presented with a medal, just as Mr. James had guessed he
would be. The Queen invited the Morgan family to bring
Tecwyn to the next garden party at Buckingham Palace.

Later that day, when the royal cars had left, and all

the mothers had gone home to talk about the wonderful clothes the Queen had worn, a huge brass sign was put up at the entrance of the main building: "Royal Pennyben Atomic Power Station."

Tecwyn was proud and happy and coal strikes no longer bothered him. He only ate an occasional lump just for fun as a human might eat candy. He had to be tested regularly to make sure that there was no danger of radiation coming from him, but his scales were now so strong and healthy that there was never any trouble of that kind.

Many villages in Wales asked for his help, particularly in winter; but he always saw to the needs of the people of Pennyben first.

The village of Pennyben became famous all over the world, partly because of its atomic power station which had been opened by the Queen. But, of course, everyone knew that the *real* reason was that—one day, in a valley deep in the heart of the Welsh mountains, a dragon was born.